Contents

Black Bones

by

E. E. Richardson

In memory of my mother

First American edition published in 2012 by Stoke Books,
an imprint of Barrington Stoke Ltd

18 Walker Street, Edinburgh, United Kingdom, EH3 7LP

www.stokebooks.com

A catalog record for this book is available from
the US Library of Congress

Distributed in the United States and Canada by Lerner Publisher
Services, a division of Lerner Publishing Group, Inc.

241 First Avenue North, Minneapolis, MN 55401

www.lernerbooks.com

ISBN 978-1-78112-100-9

Printed in China

Chapter 1

The Skull in the Box

There was a skull on Tony's desk when he got to work.

At first, he didn't know that was what it was. The skull was in a plain brown box. It looked like any other package that might come into the shop. He made a cup of coffee before he opened it.

When he took the lid off, he saw the skull.

It was the shape of a human skull, but he could see that it wasn't human. The teeth

1

were too sharp. The bones were black, not white. And it had big curly horns, like a ram's.

Tony looked at it for a bit. "Huh," he said. Then he got up and went into the front room of the shop.

The shop was still and empty at this time of day. It was just past two-thirty in the afternoon. Most of the shop's customers only came in after dark.

It was Tony's father's shop, and it sold magic. Not just card tricks and fake wands. The real thing.

The front room of the shop was packed with stuff. There were old books stacked up all over the floor. Rows of jars and bottles around the walls. There was a glass case full of silver rings, and a wall hung with mirrors.

And those were just the most normal-looking things.

Some of the things Tony's dad sold made the skull look nice. But his dad wasn't here right now. He was off on a world tour, looking for new kinds of spells. He'd been gone for two weeks.

So where had the skull come from?

Tony went over to the front till. There was only one shop assistant. She was a part-time art student called Jazz. She had blue hair and at least three tattoos.

"Hey, Jazz," Tony said.

"Yeah?" Jazz didn't look up from the till.

"You know my birthday's not till June, right?" he said.

She just looked puzzled. "Huh?"

Tony gave a sigh. "Why is there a skull on my desk?" he asked.

"Is it a skull?" Jazz said with a blank look.

"It's a skull," he said. "A black one. With horns."

"Well, it's not from me," she said. "Some woman left it for you."

He tried to think who would leave him an evil skull. "Was it one of my ex-girlfriends?" he asked.

Jazz let out a snort. "Ha. No way," she said. "She had far too much class to go out with you."

"Hey, I have class," Tony said. "I have lots of class."

"Yeah, right. Sure you do." Jazz rolled her eyes. She held up a printed card. "She left this."

Tony took the card and read it. It said –

Robin Smith

Folk Tales and Story-Telling

Reed College

He knew where Reed College was. It was on the other side of town. But he didn't know Robin Smith.

"Never heard of her," he said with a frown. "Why would a woman I don't know leave me a skull?"

Jazz gave a bored shrug. "Don't ask me," she said. "I just work here."

There was a phone number on the card. Tony went back into the office to look for his cell phone. He had to dig around in the piles of junk to find it.

It turned out to be under a T-shirt on the floor. He picked it up and called the number on the card.

"Hello?" said a woman's voice.

"Hi, this is Tony," he said. "Um, do I know you?"

The woman didn't answer right away. "This is Robin," she said at last. "Do I know *you?*"

Tony put his feet up on the desk next to the skull. "Well, I don't know," he said, looking at it. "Do you give black skulls to a lot of people?"

"Oh!" the woman said. "You're from the magic shop? Sorry. I asked the girl at the till to give it to Mr. Kim." She sounded annoyed.

"I'm Tony Kim," he said. He sat back with a sigh. "But I've got a feeling that maybe you wanted my dad."

"You're Henry Kim's son?" she said. "Oh, I see. Look, I'm sorry to be a pain, but is he there? I need to talk to him as soon as possible."

"Ah. Well, that could be a problem," Tony said. "He's not in the shop right now."

"Well, when will he be back?" she said. Her voice was a bit sharp.

"In a few weeks," Tony said.

"Oh," she said. Then she said, "Damn."

Tony did his best not to laugh. It wasn't easy. "Um, listen," he said. "If it's that important, can I help? I'm not my dad, but I know a few things."

There was a long silence. The woman must have been thinking hard. "All right," she said in the end. "I guess that's the best offer I'm going to get. Do you have any idea what that thing is?"

Tony poked the skull with a pen. "Nope," he said. "But it looks like black magic to me."

"Me too." Her voice was grim. "It was left at the college where I work last night. Some men in long cloaks and hoods were doing a chant round it. They left in a hurry when a load of people turned up for a basketball game. Maybe that scared them off."

Men in cloaks? Oh, boy. That didn't sound good.

Tony stood up. "OK," he said into the phone. "I'm on my way."

Chapter 2

Reed College

Tony took the skull with him when he left. He put it in his backpack with his magic kit.

"I'm going out for a bit," he told Jazz. "I don't know when I'll be back."

"OK," Jazz said. "I'll try to cope with the crowds on my own." The two of them were the only ones in the shop. "Don't forget you've got to take Max his spell later," she added.

"Oh, is it the full moon tonight?" Tony looked up at the moon chart on the wall.

Max was a werewolf. He got the same spell from the shop at each full moon. It was to make him look like a fox instead of a wolf.

"All right. I won't forget," Tony said. "I'll do it when I get back."

"OK," Jazz said. "See you later."

Tony went out to get on his motorcycle.

Reed College was out on the edge of town. Tony drove past it a lot, but he'd never been in. He rode his bike over there and parked in front of the gates.

The college was old. The buildings were made of dark red bricks. There was even a statue on the lawn. It was a tree trunk carved into the shape of a man.

Tony wasn't sure who it was meant to be. A lot of the carving had worn off. Now it was just a man with no face.

In fact, the whole place looked a bit run down. It could all use a good wash and some fresh paint.

There were students everywhere. None of them looked twice at Tony. With the bag on his back, he must have looked like one of them.

He went looking for Robin Smith.

She'd told him what room to come to. It still took him a long time to find it. The room numbers were all over the place. None of them were in the right order.

At last Tony found Robin Smith's room. He knocked on the door. It was opened by a young black woman in a red suit. "Can I help you?" she said.

She didn't sound like she'd been waiting for him. But it was the same voice as on the phone. She had to be Robin Smith.

"That depends," he said. He opened the zip on his bag to show the skull. "Is this guy a friend of yours?"

Robin stared at him. "*You're* Tony Kim?" she said, as if it was hard to believe.

Tony gave her a shrug. "Who did you want? Brad Pitt?" he said.

"How *old* are you?" she asked.

"I'm seventeen," he said.

"Oh, that's just great," Robin said with a groan.

"Hey, I know things!" Tony said. He folded his arms. "I know lots of things. My dad's been teaching me magic all my life."

"I'm sorry," she said. She didn't sound like she meant it. "It's just that I've met your dad. He must be, what, 65 by now? So I did think you'd be a bit ... older."

"He was a slow starter," Tony said. It was odd to think about the fact that his mom and dad had once been a couple. They'd split up when Tony was small. His mom lived in London now and he didn't see her much. She didn't like magic.

"Look, do you want my help or not?" he asked Robin.

"Fine," Robin said with a sigh. "I guess you can't make things worse." She stood to one side to let him into the room.

It was her office. The room was small, with a lot of books. There was a glass case full of art from around the world.

Tony stood the skull on the desk. He bent down to look into its eyes.

"So where did you get this thing?" he asked Robin.

"It was left in front of the statue of Doctor Reed," she said.

"That big wooden thing on the front lawn?" Tony said. Robin nodded. "Who was he?"

"The man who set up the college," she told him.

That made sense. Doctor Reed was at the heart of the college. His statue would be a good thing to put a spell on. That way the spell would work on the whole college.

Tony looked up at Robin. "Do you know who might want to put a curse on the college?" he asked.

She frowned. "It's a college, Mr. Kim," she said. "We give students low marks when they don't do the work. But other than that, we don't make a lot of enemies."

"Call me Tony," he said. He brushed dust off his knees as he stood up. "Right. I'll cast some spells, see if I can work out what this thing is meant to do."

Robin put her hands on her hips. "Are you sure you know what you're doing?" she said.

"Of course I do," Tony said. "I deal with curses all the time."

That was sort of true. They did take curses off things at the shop. But most of those were small and simple spells.

Tony looked at the black skull again. It didn't look like it was part of a simple spell.

He could be in over his head here.

Chapter 3
Fairy Dust

"OK," Tony said. "I'm going to cast a spell that shows where there's any magic. It'll let us know if there's any sort of curse on the skull."

He got some candles out of his bag. They were long and thin, black at the base and white at the top. He stood four of them round the skull.

"Can you turn the light off?" he asked Robin. "Oh, and close those blinds, too."

She did as he asked. It made the room dim, but not really dark.

Tony lit the candles with a match. The flames that they cast looked black and white too. They seemed to suck all the color out of the room.

Robin blinked her eyes a few times. "What's in those candles?" she asked him.

Tony gave a small grin. "Magic," he said.

He pulled a glass jar out of his bag. It was full of silver dust, like glitter. As soon as he took it out of the bag, it started to glow.

"What's that?" Robin asked.

"Fairy dust," Tony said. "It reacts to magic."

"Fairy dust," Robin said. "For real?"

"Yeah. From real fairies," Tony said. "They're not like the ones you see in books. They don't look like Barbie dolls with wings. They're more like bugs. They glow in the dark, and they can copy voices. They like to try and trick people."

"So how do you get the dust?" she asked.

"Trap some fairies in a jar until they die," he said.

Robin made a face. "That's horrible!"

"Yeah?" Tony gave her a look. "You know what fairies like to do for fun? They find dark roads and fly up to look like street lights. They try to get people to drive off the road and get killed."

He tipped some of the dust out into his hand.

"Fairies are not nice," he said as he put the jar back down. "A lot of magic is not nice. There are a lot of ways that it can hurt you." Tony looked down at the skull. "So let's find out what this thing is. It doesn't look nice either."

He held the dust out in front of him. Then he closed his eyes and said the words of the spell.

"Let all the hidden things be clear.
Let all secrets be known.
If any spells have been cast here,
Then let them now be shown!"

Tony blew on the dust in his hands. It floated out and hung in the air in a cloud. Then it slowly sank down. As the specks of dust hit the skull, their glow went out.

"Huh," Tony said, when the dust was all gone. "That's odd." He was sure the spell should have showed *something*.

Robin put her hands on her hips. "What does that mean?" she said. "There's no magic in the skull? So there isn't a curse on it?"

"I don't know," Tony said with a frown. He bent down to peer at the skull. "Maybe it didn't work right. I guess the next step is to – whoa!"

He jumped back as the eyes of the skull lit up.

It wasn't the silver glow of fairy dust. It was a dull, dark red like blood.

The skull shot up off the desk to float in mid air. It turned from side to side, as if it was looking around the room. Then it faced the two of them and spoke.

"Who dares to wake me from my sleep?" it said. Its voice was loud as thunder.

Tony gulped. He looked at Robin, but it didn't look like she would be much help. She was staring at the skull as if it would bite.

He hoped it wouldn't.

"Er, we did," he said in a weak voice.

"Fools!" the skull said. "The hour of the blood moon draws near. Soon I will walk in this world again. I will feast on the bodies of the dead! The streets will run with blood. All who do not serve me will die!"

Tony took a step back. "Er ... cool," he said. He put on a fake smile. "That sounds great."

He didn't think it would be smart to make this thing angry. But they needed to find out what was going on.

"So, um, you're coming back to this world?" he said. "That must take some strong magic. Can you tell us about the spell? Just so we can make sure it gets done right," he lied.

The skull's eyes lit up like tiny suns. "Silence!" it said. "Do you think I will fall for your tricks? You seek to stop my return. But it cannot be stopped. At the night of the blood moon, I will rise!"

The skull's mouth fell open. A blast of cold air blew out.

It was like being hit by a snow storm. The wind tore at Tony's hair and clothes. It was so cold it made his skin hurt. It was like being scraped with a razor.

And the skull just kept on blowing. Frost had started to form on the walls. The carpet was going white. Tony grabbed Robin by the arm.

"We've got to get out of here!" he yelled. They ran out into the hallway. Tony slammed the door shut behind them.

"How long will that door hold it?" Robin asked.

Tony looked down. He could see frost creeping under the door.

"Not long!" he said.

Chapter 4
Ice Storm

Ice had formed in all the gaps around the door. Tony could hear the wood creak and groan. Soon the ice would be too much and force the door open.

And then they would be in big trouble.

"What *is* that thing in there?" Robin asked.

"There's some kind of spirit in the skull," Tony said. "My spell must have woken it up. If we're lucky, it's just an imp. They like to scare people, but they're not all that strong."

"And if we're *not* lucky?" she said. "What if it's not just an imp?"

Tony's face was grim. "Then it's a demon," he said.

Imps were just pests. They could do some harm, but they were easy to chase off. But demons had a lot of power. And they were pure evil. All they wanted to do was kill.

"Can you get rid of it?" Robin asked.

"I'll try!" Tony put his hands on the door. It was so cold that it hurt to touch. He could feel his skin stick to it.

He tried to think of the words to send a spirit away. His dad had made him learn all of the spells. But it was hard to think with the howling wind.

"Evil spirit, hear me!" he said.
"I send you from this place.
Return to where you came from,
And do not leave a trace.
I break the chains that hold you.
I set you free to roam.
I cast you out of this world.
Now return to your home!"

Tony shouted the last words. As the noise faded away, everything went quiet. The wind had stopped.

"Is it gone?" Robin asked.

"There's only one way to find out," Tony said. He took hold of the door handle and pulled it open.

And saw the skull floating in the air in front of him. Its red eyes lit up again.

"Crap!" Tony slammed the door shut just in time. The blast of frost that hit it nearly blew it open again. He had to hold it shut with his own body.

He could hear the wood starting to crack. It wouldn't hold up for much longer.

He gave Robin a weak smile. "Well," he said. "At least now we know it's not an imp."

"Now what?" she shouted over the sound of the wind.

"Now I try again!" Tony shut his eyes and tried to think.

The thing in the skull had to be a demon. It was too strong for him to send away. But maybe he could get it to go back to sleep. If he could just think of the right spell …

Got it! "Restless spirit, be at peace!" he said.

"No longer be a pest.

Leave behind the living world,

and go back to your rest!"

This time there was a small thud from the other side of the door. Tony looked at Robin. They both held still for a few seconds. Nothing moved or made a sound.

Tony pulled the door open. This time he did it slowly.

The skull was on the carpet. Tony poked it with his foot. It didn't move, so he gave it a harder push. It rolled over, and he saw the red light was gone from his eyes.

"OK," he said. He let out a big huff of breath. "I think that did it."

He looked up from the skull for the first time. The room looked like an ice cave. There was frost on all the books. The walls were thick with ice. Even the candles had frozen.

"Whoa," he said. "Er ... I think you might need to move out of this office for a while. Sorry."

Robin's eyes were still on the skull. "So is that thing safe now?" she asked. "Did you get rid of the demon?"

Tony shook his head. "No," he said. "It's still in the skull. I just put it back to sleep."

Robin took a step back. "How long before it wakes up?" she asked.

Tony bent down to pick up the skull. "It shouldn't wake up on its own," he said. "Only if someone casts a spell on it."

"Then don't do any more spells!" she said.

Tony looked up at her. "I won't," he said. "But someone else might. Those guys in the cloaks must have been trying to wake the demon up." He pulled a face. "Or worse."

"What's worse?" Robin asked.

"You heard what the skull said. It will walk in this world again at the blood moon. What if they're trying to bring it back to life?" he said.

"How bad would that be?" Robin asked.

"At the moment, the demon's weak," Tony told her. "It's just a spirit. It can't leave the place where the skull is. And it can only do small spells. If it had all its magic, we'd be dead by now."

Robin crossed her arms. "Well, who would want to bring it back to life?" she said. "That's crazy!"

"It's probably some kind of cult," he said. "A group of people who want to bring the demon back. They must think the demon will help them. But they're wrong. Once it's got a new body, it won't need them any more. They'll get killed, just like everyone else."

"So how do we stop them?" Robin asked.

"I don't know," Tony said. "But I guess I'd better find out. Fast."

Chapter 5
Max

Tony took the skull away with him when he left Reed College. He didn't think it was smart to leave it there. What if the men who'd left it came back?

When he got back to the shop he went over to his dad's safe.

The safe was in the back wall of the office. It was made of three metal boxes – one inside another. The first one was made of iron. Then silver. Then copper. Each one had spells cast on it. When the safe door was shut, no magic could get in – or out.

Tony put the skull in the safe. Then he poured a ring of salt round the skull, just in case. Salt helped to block spells.

He shut the safe door, and took a deep breath.

The demon should stay asleep in there – for now. But he didn't know what would happen at the blood moon.

He didn't even know when that was. Was it the full moon? The half moon? This month? Next month?

Tony stared at his dad's books on the wall. There were rows and rows of them. Most of them were so old that they were written by hand. It could take days to look things up in them. What if he didn't have that much time?

A knock on the office door made him jump. Jazz opened it and stuck her head in. "Hey, Tony," she said. "Are you going to take this spell to Max or what?"

Tony stared at her. Then he gave a wide grin. "Jazz!" he said. "You're a genius. I'll go and see Max!"

Max was a werewolf. He must know all about the moon. He would surely know when the blood moon was.

Tony ran to get his coat.

"Hey, wait!" Jazz shouted after him. "Don't forget to take the spell with you!"

Max's house was on the east side of town. Tony knew how to find it. He'd been there lots of times.

The spell to make Max look like a fox had to be made fresh each month. But Max got ill when it was close to the full moon. It was hard for him to come into the shop, so Tony took the spells to him instead.

Most days, he would just put the spell in the letter box. But today he had to talk to Max. He went up to the door and rang the bell.

No one came to the door. But Tony was sure he heard a creak inside the house. He rang the bell again.

"Hello?" he shouted. "Max? It's Tony Kim from the magic shop."

It took a long time for Max to come to the door. When he did, he only opened it a crack.

"What do you want?" Max said. His voice was low. It sounded like his throat hurt. "I've paid for the spell."

"I know," Tony said. He held up the spell. It was a bag full of fox fur and a few other things. "I've got it right here. I just need to speak to you."

"Can it wait?" Max said. "This is not a good time."

"I know, I'm sorry," Tony said. "But it's important."

Max took a few steps back from the door. "Come in, then," he said. "And shut the door behind you."

Max moved to the far end of the hall as Tony came in. All the lights were off in the house. Max's eyes must be hurting.

He looked terrible. His skin was pale and sweaty, and there were shadows under his eyes.

As Tony shut the door, he felt nervous. He knew it was stupid. The moon wasn't up yet. And even if it was, Max wouldn't hurt him. A werewolf was like a real wolf. It wouldn't pick a fight for no reason.

All the same, he wanted to get this over with fast.

He gave a weak smile. "I just wanted to ask you if you know when the blood moon is," he said.

Max stared at him. "That's all?" he said. "It's the first full moon after the harvest. It's tonight."

Tony felt like his stomach had just done a flip. "Crap," he said in a small voice.

Max folded his arms. "Is that it?" he asked. "Can I have my spell now?"

"Oh, yeah, sorry." Tony moved to hand the bag to Max.

As he held it out, Max grabbed him by the wrist. He gave Tony's arm a long, slow sniff. Then he let out a deep growl.

"You stink of black magic," Max said, in a harsh voice. "It's all over you." He stared at Tony again. His eyes were yellow. Hadn't they been blue a second ago?

And had his teeth always been that sharp?

Tony pulled his hand back. His heart was beating fast in his chest. "Um, yeah," he said. He gave a nervous laugh. "It's not mine! See, there was this skull, and – "

Max let out a snarl. As he did, his face seemed to stretch. His jaw grew longer. His teeth got bigger. The hands that stuck out from his sleeves became paws. Pale fur burst out all over his body.

Tony heard bones crack and crunch as Max dropped down to his hands and knees. The shape of his body was changing. And it was doing it *fast*.

Tony turned and ran for the door.

31

Chapter 6
Two Tonys

It felt like the hall had gotten longer. Tony was sure he'd only walked a few steps when he'd come in. But now the front door seemed to be a mile away.

He looked back over his shoulder as he ran. What he saw nearly made him trip.

Max was no longer human at all. In his place was a massive white wolf. It was crouched down, ready to spring.

"Whoa!" Tony's eyes went wide in panic. Still looking back, he ran right into the door. "Ow!"

He slapped at the door, trying to find the handle. He didn't dare turn his back on the wolf. It could jump at any moment.

The wolf let out a growl that made the hairs on Tony's neck stand up. He saw its legs go tense …

And then his fingers found the door handle. He turned it and yanked hard.

Tony didn't wait for the door to get all the way open. He just shoved his way out of the gap as soon as he could.

As he fell out into the street, he heard the wolf jump. It hit the door with a thud that made the glass rattle.

The gap was too small for it to get out. But one big white paw came round the side of the door. It was trying to pull it open.

Tony pulled on the door from the other side, trying to get it shut. The wolf let out a yelp as its paw was crushed in the gap. It drew the paw back, and Tony pulled at the door again. This time it slammed shut.

He heard the wolf's claws scrape at the door. It didn't have hands to turn the handle. It was trapped.

All the same, Tony ran to get on his bike as fast as he could.

His heart didn't slow down until he was a mile away. His arm had started to throb where he'd hit the door. He knew he was lucky not to have been hurt worse.

Why had Max gone for him like that? He must have smelled the demon on him. Tony couldn't smell it, but his nose wasn't as good as a wolf's.

It had to be bad to make Max lose control like that. It was as if he hadn't known who Tony was. He'd just smelled evil and tried to attack.

Now Tony had left, the wolf should calm down. It wouldn't try to come after him.

But that didn't mean Tony was safe. Max had said the blood moon was tonight. And it wouldn't be long before the sun set.

Tony only had a few hours. He had to find out who was trying to call up that demon. And then he had to find a way to stop them.

He parked his motorcycle and went into the shop. Jazz gave him a funny look as he came in.

"What did you do that for?" she asked him with a frown.

All Tony had done was walk in the door. "What did I do *what* for?" he asked.

"Come back in again. Did you just climb out of the window in your office and then come back in around the front?" Jazz said. She was looking at him as if he was crazy.

She was the one who was crazy here. "Er, *no*," Tony said. He pointed at the door. "I went out the front door half an hour ago. You saw me do it! I've just got back."

Jazz glared at him. "Tony, I *saw* you come back in just now," she said. "You went into the office a few minutes ago!"

"No I didn't!" he said. "I was all the way across town, having a fight with a werewolf!"

"Then who the hell is in your office?" Jazz said.

They both turned to look at the office door. "That's a good question," Tony said slowly.

Tony made his way across the shop to the closed door. He stood in front of it for a few seconds. There was no sound from inside.

He yanked it open.

There was a man in the office. He was standing in front of the safe. The door had been ripped off, and he was just reaching in for the skull.

"Hey!" Tony said. The man spun round with the skull in his hands.

But that wasn't what made Tony stare.

The man had Tony's *face*. It was like looking in a mirror. He had the same nose. The same chin. The same haircut. The same body.

Only one thing was wrong – the eyes. Tony's eyes were dark brown. But this man's eyes were black. *All* black – the whites of his eyes, too.

There were all kinds of spells that could make your body look different. But there was no kind of magic that could change your eyes.

Tony had to look away for a second. It was just too freaky. As he did, he saw the pot of salt on the desk. He'd left it there after putting some around the skull.

Salt could break spells.

He grabbed the pot of salt and tore the lid off. Then he threw salt all over the man who looked like him.

It was like watching a stone drop into water. Where the salt hit the man, his shape seemed to ripple. His body grew longer. His face changed. His skin changed color.

By the time the spell was gone, he didn't look like Tony at all.

In fact, he didn't even look human.

Chapter 7
The Magic Map

The thing in front of Tony was not a man at all. It had grey, bumpy skin and sharp teeth. On top of its head were two horns that looked just as sharp.

It was a troll. And it was bigger than Tony. A *lot* bigger.

Tony took a step back.

"Er, hi," he said, with a weak grin. He held up his hands. "Um ... sorry about the salt. I hope that didn't hurt. Salt isn't bad for trolls, right?"

The troll let out a snarl. "You dare to try and stop the Great One from rising?" it said. "He will feast on your dead flesh and drink your blood!"

"Yeah. He already told me that." Tony tried to sound bold. "Now, put the skull down. Or I'll use my magic on you."

It was a bluff. There wasn't a lot that could hurt a troll. Their skin was as hard as rock. Tony didn't know any spells that would work.

He just hoped the troll didn't know that.

The troll growled and Tony saw all its teeth. "You cannot harm me," it said. "The power of the Great One protects me!"

It bent down, aimed its head at Tony and ran at him.

"Whoa!" Tony yelled and jumped out of the way. Those horns could rip him open. He looked round the room for a weapon.

But the troll didn't stop to fight. It ran right past him and out into the shop. He heard a crash from the front room. Jazz screamed.

Tony ran out into the front room. The troll was headed for the door with the skull. It didn't bother to walk around things. It just smashed them out of the way.

The mess it had made got in his way as he ran after it. He had to jump over all the books and broken glass.

By the time he got to the door, it was too late. The troll was gone.

Tony didn't bother to chase it. The troll could have cast a new spell by now. There was no way to know what it would look like this time.

He went back into the shop.

Jazz was picking things up off the floor. "What the hell was that thing?" she asked.

"A troll," Tony said. He gave a tired sigh.

The troll had got away with the skull. Now it could call up the demon. And Tony was the only one who had a chance to stop it.

He just had to work out how.

Tony looked at his watch. It was after five o'clock. He was running out of time.

"Some help would be nice," Jazz said. She pulled a face at the mess. "It's going to take hours to sort all this stuff out. And half of it's broken. What's this bottle of green stuff? It stinks."

"Who knows?" Tony said with a shrug. He didn't care that much right now. The state of the shop was the least of his problems.

But then her words sank in. And gave him an idea.

The green stuff wasn't the only thing that gave off a stink. Max had been able to smell the evil from the skull on Tony. The black magic must be really strong. It would stand out.

So if Tony could find some way to track it ...

He looked at the mess of jars and bottles on the floor. He spotted a jar full of fairy dust. It hadn't broken like the rest. He picked it up and headed for the office.

"Oh, thanks, Tony," Jazz said. She rolled her eyes. "That was a lot of help. You do one jar, I'll do the rest, right?"

"If you could, that'd be great," Tony said. He gave her a thumbs up. "Thanks, Jazz!" He went into the office.

He cleared all the stuff off the desk. Then he got out a street map of the town.

It wasn't just a normal map. His dad had drawn it by hand. It showed things no other map did. There were all kinds of spells cast on it.

Tony spread the map out on top of the desk. Then he tipped some fairy dust out into his hands. He held it out over the map and spoke the words of the tracking spell.

"Show me north, south, east and west," he said.

"Show me up and down.

Show me where the magic lies,

All around this town!"

On the last word, he pulled his hands apart. He let the fairy dust fall down over the map.

It didn't just fall. The dust spun round in the air. It was as if the wind was blowing it. But there was no wind in the room.

Specks of dust landed on the street map. Tony could see that it wasn't just random. There were patterns in the way it fell.

On some parts of the map there was no dust at all. In others there were small piles. Places in the town where magic could be found.

There were three spots where the dust was thickest. One was the shop. One was Reed College.

And one was a road on the other side of town. Bow Street.

Tony gave a small, thin smile. "Got you, Mr. Troll," he said.

Chapter 8
A Nest of Trolls

Tony rode his motorcycle at well over the speed limit. There was no time to lose. He had less than an hour before the sun went down.

He parked at the end of Bow Street. This part of town was a dump. There'd been a row of shops here once. But now most of them were closed and boarded up.

Tony walked down the street. When he was one shop from the end, he saw it. The shop had wooden planks over its windows like the others, but one of the planks was loose.

He went over to it and pulled it. Then he peeked into the empty shop.

The first thing that hit him was the smell. It was like old socks and rotting meat. He could see little bones all over the floor. The trolls must have been eating birds and rats.

There were heaps of dirty rags too. They were in three piles. Beds for three trolls?

It didn't look like any of them were home.

Tony took a deep breath, and pushed in past the board.

For a moment he was sure he was going to be sick. But then the smell got a bit better. His nose must be getting used to it.

He still had the jar of fairy dust with him. He took it out, and it started to glow.

Now he could see that the walls were covered in troll writing. It looked like it was painted in blood. Tony just hoped that it wasn't *human* blood.

He couldn't read the troll words, but there were pictures too. He tried to make sense of the story they told.

It looked like the trolls had been the demon's servants. They'd helped it to fight humans – but in the end, the humans had won. They'd used some kind of spell to burn the demon. All that was left were the bones.

The humans had taken the skull, but the trolls had picked up the rest of the bones. There was one picture of them in front of a statue. Was it the one at Reed College?

The trolls must have hidden the bones there. And they'd been waiting a long time till they could get the skull back. If they had the skull, then they could put it together with the bones and call up the demon.

And now they had it. They'd tried to get the bones last night at Reed College, but the basketball team had scared them off. They must not have wanted to be seen. They'd have to go back there tonight and try again.

Tony was in the wrong place.

He swore and left the nest at a run.

Tony got out his phone as he headed for his bike. He called Robin's number. It seemed to take an age for her to pick up.

"Hello?" her voice said at last.

"Robin! It's Tony Kim. Are you still at the college?" he asked.

"Yes," she said. "I was just about to – "

"There's no time!" Tony said. He got on his bike. "The blood moon is *tonight*. The trolls are coming there. They – "

"Wait, *trolls?*" she said. "What are you talking about?"

"They're the ones who are doing the spell to get the demon back!" he shouted. "They're coming to the college. The rest of the demon's bones are there. We haven't got much time. The moon will be up in half an hour. I'm going to go back to the shop and – "

"Tony!" Robin cut in. "The moon's not going to be up in half an hour."

"What?" he said.

"Look at the *sky*," she said.

Tony looked up – and felt his guts go cold.

"Oh, crap," he said in a small voice.

He'd got it wrong. He'd been counting down the time till the sun set. But the sun set and the moon rose at *different times*.

They didn't have half an hour till the blood moon rose.

It was already up in the sky.

He shoved his phone in his pocket and drove off.

Tony rode the bike as fast as it would go. Car horns honked as he zipped past them. At least two speed cameras flashed.

That didn't matter. He'd be happy to pay the fines in a few days' time.

To pay them, he'd have to be *alive*.

By the time he made it to the college, the sun was on its way down. Everything was dark. The students must have gone home by now. He guessed most of the staff had too.

That was good. Not so many people around who could get hurt.

Of course, if the trolls called up the demon, no one would be safe.

Tony left his bike at the gates. It was hard to see much in the shadows. There was a tall shape ahead that must be the statue of Doctor Reed. He headed for it.

And then the shape *moved*. Tony let out of a gasp of surprise –

And a hand was clapped over his mouth.

Tony tried to fight as he was dragged backwards. His elbow hit something soft, and there was a yelp.

Wait. That didn't feel *or* sound like a troll ...

"Stop it, you idiot!" a voice hissed in his ear. It was Robin. She took her hand off of his mouth. "There are three of those troll things here," she told him. "They just pulled down the statue of Doctor Reed."

"The bones must be buried under it," Tony said. He took a deep breath. "OK. That's good. If they have to dig, then we still have some time."

No sooner had he said it than there was a flare of bright white light. A massive boom like thunder filled the air.

Chapter 9
Spell Fire

Tony had to shut his eyes to block out the light. When it had dimmed down a bit, he took a look.

One of the trolls was now holding a burning torch. But it was far too bright to be normal fire.

"What's that?" Robin asked in a whisper.

"Spell fire," Tony told her. "It's the hottest kind of flame you can make with magic." But why would the trolls need a fire that hot?

The spell fire had made the college as bright as day. Tony was glad Robin had dragged him back to the gates. They could hide behind them.

Not that the trolls were looking their way. There were three of them, all in cloaks. They stood round the statue, which was now lying flat on the grass.

What were they doing?

Tony could hear a low sound. It was like a hum, but made up of grunts and snarls. It was the trolls. They were chanting the words of a spell.

Robin poked him in the side. "What's going on?" she asked.

"I don't know," Tony said.

As they watched, the statue began to float up in the air. It rose up a couple of feet, then stopped.

The troll with the torch moved forward. It touched the flame to the wooden statue.

The statue went up in flames right away. It burned as fast as oil. One second there was a statue. The next there were just falling ashes.

No, wait. That wasn't quite true. The wood had all burned away … but something was still left. Thin, dark shapes floated in the air. Like metal rods, or …

Black bones.

"Holy crap," Tony said. The demon's bones weren't buried in the ground. They'd been hidden in the statue.

And now the trolls had the whole set. Another troll stepped up with the skull. It put it where the statue's head had been. It stayed hanging there in mid air.

The trolls started to chant again. Two of them were speaking in troll grunts. The third one chanted words in English.

"Bones to flesh.
Life from death.
Heart takes beats.
Lungs take breath.
Ears that hear.
Eyes with sight.
Claws that rip.
Teeth that bite."

The words went on and on. The fast beat of the chant was like the sound of a train. It made the hair on the back of Tony's neck stand up.

The black bones had started to glow. There was a blood red cloud around them. The body of the demon was taking shape.

Robin had a tight grip on Tony's arm. "We have to stop them!" she said.

"I *know!*" Tony said. But how? He hadn't had time to go back to the shop. He had nothing magic on him.

No, wait. That wasn't quite true. He still had the jar of fairy dust.

And now he had an idea.

"What are you doing?" Robin asked as he pulled the jar out of his pocket.

"No time to explain!" He ran at the trolls with the jar.

They didn't turn to look at him. They were too focused on the spell. Even hitting them might not distract them. Their skin was too thick to feel it.

So as he drew his arm back to throw the jar, he didn't aim at the trolls. Instead, he flung the jar at the floating bones.

The glass jar hit the skull and broke into tiny pieces. Silver dust flew out. It mixed with the red glow of the trolls' spell.

The trolls were casting a spell that was meant to bring dead things back to life. Would it work on fairies too?

A ball of silver light rose up from the bones. Then another one. Then more and more, faster and faster. It was like seeing popcorn pop.

The lights zipped around the sky like bugs. Tony could hear the sound of giggles in the air.

"What are they?" Robin asked. She stared up at the swirl of lights.

"Fairies!" he said. "Get down!" He grabbed her arm and pulled her down to the ground.

"What?" she said. "Why do we need to – ?"

That was when the fairies dived down out of the sky.

They flew down at the trolls all at once, like a flock of birds. They tore at the trolls' cloaks and pulled their horns. They grabbed at the bones and tried to fly away with them.

The trolls tried to keep chanting, but it was no good. The fairies were small, but there were dozens of them. There were too many to swat away. Their giggles had turned to happy screams, like kids on a theme park ride.

Tony saw the red glow round the bones start to thin out. The magic was running out. The trolls would have to start the spell again.

He wasn't going to give them the chance. "Come on!" he yelled at Robin. "We've got to get that skull back!"

They ran into the cloud of fairies.

It was like running into a strong wind. Fairies pulled at his hair and tore his clothes. They pinched his skin and poked him in the eyes. The silver lights were so bright, it hurt to look at them.

One of the trolls stood on Tony's foot. He let out a yell, but then an elbow hit him in the gut. He couldn't see what was going on. Where was the skull?

"I've got it!" Robin shouted. Then she let out a scream of surprise. "Tony!"

Chapter 10
Broken Bones

Tony could see that Robin had a grip on the skull – but so did one of the trolls. It only had one hand on the skull, because it was still holding the torch in the other. All the same, it was winning the tug-of-war.

Tony ran to help. He and Robin both pulled on the skull. But the troll had a solid grip now. It wasn't letting go.

The troll let out a sharp grunt – an order to the other trolls. They both came running.

And then the fairies got in on the act.

Seeing the fight over the skull, they all dived down on it. They might not know what the skull was, but they could see that people wanted it.

And fairies loved to steal things.

Two of them flew into the skull's eye sockets. They lifted it up from inside. More of them pulled at Tony's fingers. He lost his grip on the skull.

The fairies rose up and up into the sky with it. They danced around in the air, giggling.

The troll with the torch gave a snarl of anger. It held its free hand up and started to chant. Tony couldn't make sense of the words.

But he heard the fairies scream. They let go of the skull and flew off in all directions.

The skull didn't fall. A red glow had sprung up round it. As the troll kept on chanting, it floated down slowly.

"Do something!" Robin said. She grabbed his arm.

Tony didn't know *what* to do. How could he fight the trolls? He had no magic with him.

And the kinds of spells he knew off by heart were no good. They were all simple things. Just small party tricks.

But maybe a trick was all that he would need. Tony's eyes fixed on the troll's torch. He held out his hand and shouted the words of a spell.

"Fire blaze. Fire burn.

See the flames that twist and turn.

Fire strong. Fire bright.

Fire burn with all your might!"

The flame of the torch grew to five times its size. The troll let go of it with a yelp.

As it dropped the torch, the troll broke off its chant. The red glow round the skull winked out.

And the skull fell.

It dropped out of the sky like a stone. The trolls all ran to catch it. But Tony could see they wouldn't get there in time. He took hold of Robin's arm to pull her away. "Run!" he yelled.

They both ran for the gate.

Tony dived down behind it. As he did, he heard the skull hit the ground. It wasn't just the crack of a bone breaking. It was more like a sonic boom.

He looked back in time to see a shadow burst out from the bones. It was something like light, something like smoke. But it was more than that. The shape that rose up from the cracked skull was alive.

It was the spirit of the demon. It had been trapped in the skull, and now it was free. It spread its dark wings wide and howled at the sky.

"*Free!*" it said, in a voice like thunder. "Free at last!"

Robin grabbed Tony's hand. Her grip was so hard he was sure she would crack *his* bones. The trolls had all dropped down to kneel on the ground.

But then the demon's wings stopped spreading. In fact, it was starting to shrink.

"What is this?" the demon said. It turned its head to stare down at the trolls. "You fools!

The spell is not complete! I cannot stay in this world without a body!"

It let out a roar. It was mad with anger. The trolls jumped up to run. But before they could get away, the demon wrapped its dark wings round them. They were pulled into its shadowy shape.

A shape that kept on shrinking. In a few seconds, it was down to the size of a car. Then a phone booth. Then a football.

And then it was just gone. Tony heard one last angry cry. It trailed off, as if the demon was falling down a deep hole. At the very end, he heard a small, soft pop.

Robin let go of his hand. "Where did it go?" she said in a whisper.

Tony stood up. "Back to the demon world," he said. He let out a breath. "And it looks like it took the trolls with it. The spell on the skull was the only thing keeping it here. Break the skull, break the spell."

Robin gave him a sharp look. "You mean you could have just dropped the skull off the top of a cliff? Would that have done the same thing?"

All of a sudden Tony felt stupid. He folded his arms. "Well – it's not like I *knew* it would work!" he said. "It might have been too strong to break!"

She stared at him. "So this whole time … you've just been making it up as you went along? You had *no* idea what you were doing?"

He gave her a wide grin. "Hey, it all worked out, didn't it?" he said with a shrug.

Robin stared at him some more. Then she let out a deep sigh, and turned to walk away.

Tony cupped his hands over his mouth to shout. "Hey!" he said. "Is this a good time to ask if I'm getting paid for this job?"

She didn't look back.